To Olivia
The heroine of the story!

Olivia Panda and her friends are playing
their best-loved game of roly poly.

It is lots
of fun and
much better
than walking.

4

Down

and down,

round and round they roll.

Bopping into each other

and bouncing off trees and bushes,

Pandas are so fluffy they never get hurt.

5

Suddenly –

SPLASH!

they roll into an unexpected puddle of water.
Where has it come from? It hasn't been raining!

As they shake the water from their fur,

Olivia can see that the nearby river has burst its banks and she wonders why.

Olivia looks downstream and notices that the river is blocked with plastic bottles and other rubbish.

"Oh no!" exclaims Olivia "the water can't get through."

"We will have to remove the rubbish, or more of the jungle could be flooded. That would be a disaster for our friends and food supply." says Olivia. But how?

9

Olivia looks around
and sees her friend
Tumble is eating
some bamboo...

...and this
gives her
an idea.

10

Olivia asks Tumble to chomp down two long lengths of bamboo,

while she tears off strips from another piece and cleverly twists the strips into a net.

11

Working together the friends make an amazing makeshift bridge.

They wonder how to get it across the water.

"I know" says the tallest stretchiest monkey, waggling his floppy hands, "I can swing across!"

Using an extra long vine and taking an extra big leap...

12

...the monkey swings safely to the other side, landing like an acrobat.

Bit by bit, Olivia and her friends push the bamboo bridge across to him. The monkey stretches out his long arms and grabs the bridge, then using some vines he ties the bamboo bridge tightly to a nearby tree.

13

Olivia carefully shimmies out onto the bridge
Being a bear, she's not
scared of climbing.

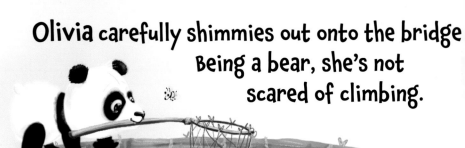

Just as she reaches the middle she loses
her grip and starts to slip!

Luckily she manages to hang on with her strong legs and sharp claws. Dangling upside down, she sees that she is close to the rubbish swirling in the water below.

Hinging on to the bridge, Olivia begins scooping up the nasty rubbish with the net.

15

The other jungle creatures all want to help, so Olivia passes the rubbish filled net to a monkey...

...who then gives it to the red panda...

...who finally hands it to the tiger!

The tiger empties the rubbish into one big pile.
"Why don't we call ourselves the Eco Crew,
as we are doing such a good job."
says the tiger. "That is a great idea."
says Olivia.

17

Finally, the last piece of rubbish is collected...

...and the river runs freely again. HOORAY!

Tumble the red panda
asks where the rubbish
came from.

Olivia
explains
that instead
of recycling it,

some people just throw their rubbish on
the ground and a lot of it ends up
in rivers and even in the SEA!

"That is terrible," says the red panda.
"We should remind everyone that –
If everybody does their bit
the planet will be fighting fit."

Olivia and the Eco Crew stand in front of the big pile of rubbish, happy with doing their bit to help.

The end